Acting Edition

Clown Bar Christmas

by Adam Szymkowicz

‖SAMUEL FRENCH‖

FOR PRODUCTION INQUIRIES

UNITED STATES AND CANADA
info@concordtheatricals.com
1-866-979-0447

UNITED KINGDOM AND EUROPE
licensing@concordtheatricals.co.uk
020-7054-7298

Each title is subject to availability from Concord Theatricals Corp.,
depending upon country of performance. Please be aware that *CLOWN
BAR CHRISTMAS* may not be licensed by Concord Theatricals Corp.
in your territory. Professional and amateur producers should contact
the nearest Concord Theatricals Corp. office or licensing partner to
verify availability.

This work is published by Samuel French, an imprint of Concord
Theatricals Corp.

MUSIC AND THIRD-PARTY MATERIALS USE NOTE

IMPORTANT BILLING AND CREDIT REQUIREMENTS

CLOWN BAR CHRISTMAS made its world premiere with the Crow River Players at the Little Theatre in New London, Minnesota, on December 21, 2023. The production was directed by Matt Hegdahl. The music director was Andrea Limoges, sound and projections were by Bethany Lacktorin, and the stage manager was Kirsten Campbell. The cast was as follows:

DUSTY	Gabriel Ryland
PETUNIA	Hope Taylor
ZIPPY	Gavin Johnson
ZULU	Acacia Banken
TIMMY	Justin Brainard
GIGGLES	Christopher Delong
SHOTGUN	Betsy Shadowick
HAPPY	John Szczur
POPO	Averi Linn
BLINKY	Nick Shadowick
OLD SPATCHY/BOBO	Thomas Lovecraft

CHARACTERS

DUSTY – male, the crooner

PETUNIA – female, the good time girl/waitress/dancer/babysitter/ bartender

ZUZU – a child clown played by an adult

ZIPPY – a child clown played by an adult

TIMMY – male, **HAPPY**'s brother, an addict. Can be doubled with **BOBO**.

GIGGLES – male, a gangster

SHOTGUN – male, a gangster

OLD SPATCHY – any gender, very old, slavic accent. Can be doubled with **BOBO**.

HAPPY – male, the leading man

BLINKY – female, the moll

POPO – female, an assassin

BOBO – male, the mob boss

SETTING

The Clown Bar, a bar full of clowns set up like a cabaret.

TIME

The present or recent past.

AUTHOR'S NOTES

This play precedes the events of the play *Clown Bar*, I'm not sure how long by. I'm not a fucking expert.

The Clown Bar is currently decorated for Christmas – maybe there's a small gaudy tree and a menorah. Maybe some clowns wear ugly sweaters or other clowny holiday outfits.

Action takes place in various audience areas and also on the small stage. Audience members are encouraged to dress like clowns. If possible, hand out clown noses to the audience along with their programs. Actors, stagehands, ushers, etc are all dressed in full clown makeup with bright hair and clown noses. Their outfits could be clowney or like gangsters from the '30s or more recent gangsters. Feel free to make guns as colorful as the clowns. Clowns may hold cliplights to illuminate scenes.

THANKS

Special thanks in no particular order to John and Rhoda Szymkowicz.

Seth Glewen, The Gersh Agency, Lily Creed, Poppy O'Hara.

Tish Dace, Kristen Palmer, Wallace Palmer Szymkowicz, Elizabeth Bochain, Betty Michel, David Michel. Vern Co. Ethan Harari. Bonnie Peters, Sharon Steflik. Ellen Morrone.

Flux Theater Ensemble and all those in Core Work, especially Corinna Schulenburg and Sienna Gonzalez.

Amy Rose Marsh, Garrett Anderson, Rachel Levens, Nate Netzley, Sarah Weber, Abbie Van Nostrand, David Geer, Ben Keiper, Emma Anacootee, Courtney Kochuba, Rosemary Bucher, and everyone at Concord Theatricals/Samuel French.

Troy Heard and Majestic Rep. Keith Claverie and everyone at the NOLA Project.

Matt Hegdahl.

Daniel Talbott and Addie Johnson, Kip Fagan, Andrew Neisler, Ari Schrier and everyone at Rising Phoenix and Pipeline who made those first Clown Bars happen.

Everyone (over 60 theaters) who decided doing *Clown Bar*, the first play, was a good idea. Without you, I never would have thought yeah let's go back to that well and see if there's anything there.

For Matt Freeman apts

*(At open, **DUSTY** has been singing a mixture of clown songs and holiday songs.)*

DUSTY. *(On the small stage.)* How's everybody doing? It's really coming down out there, huh? The snowstorm keep some of you away? That's okay. We'll work with what we got, which I guess is you clowns. You all clowns? Now's not a good time for non-clowns in the Clown Bar, even if it is the holiday season. It's too dangerous. You could catch a stray bullet or stray venereal disease. You could get a face full of seltzer or worse, fall in love with a clown. So now's the time to leave. Don't say I didn't warn you. I'll give you to the count of three. One. Two. Let's get into the holiday spirit.

(Sings to the tune of "I Saw Three Ships (Come Sailing In)" into his mic. As with most songs in the show, maybe we don't have to sing the whole thing. Maybe half or a third.)

I SAW THREE CLOWNS COME STUMBLING IN,
ON CHRISTMAS DAY, ON CHRISTMAS DAY,
I SAW THREE CLOWNS COME STUMBLING IN,
ON CHRISTMAS DAY IN THE MORNING.

AND WHO WAS WITH THOSE CLOWNS ALL THREE?
ON CHRISTMAS DAY, ON CHRISTMAS DAY,
AND WHO WAS WITH THOSE CLOWNS ALL THREE?
ON CHRISTMAS DAY IN THE MORNING.

OUR BOSS BOBO LOOKS REAL ANGRY
ON CHRISTMAS DAY, ON CHRISTMAS DAY,
OUR BOSS BOBO LOOKS REAL ANGRY
ON CHRISTMAS DAY IN THE MORNING.

AND WHAT BUMBLED THOSE CLOWNS ALL THREE?
ON CHRISTMAS DAY, ON CHRISTMAS DAY,
AND WHY DID THEY NOT TRY TO FLEE
ON CHRISTMAS DAY IN THE MORNING.

OH, THEY STROLLED INTO THE WRONG CITY,
ON CHRISTMAS DAY, ON CHRISTMAS DAY,
OH, THEY FOUGHT BUT THEN THEY BLED ON ME,
ON CHRISTMAS DAY IN THE MORNING.

AND ALL THE CLOWNS THAT DIED THAT DAY,
ON CHRISTMAS DAY, ON CHRISTMAS DAY,
AND ALL THE CLOWNS THAT DIED THAT WAY,
ON CHRISTMAS DAY IN THE MORNING.

> *(During the last part* **PETUNIA** *has entered from the back with the two clown kids,* **ZUZU** *and* **ZIPPY**. *They maybe have pigtails or breeches or those beanies with propellers – they are visually archetypal children, but also clowns.* **DUSTY** *stops singing whenever he sees them.* **PETUNIA** *sits them at a table.)*

What's this? Hey, Petunia, why did you bring kids in here? This is an inappropriate establishment for children, even clown children.

PETUNIA. Bobo doesn't like that song.

DUSTY. Yeah, I know.

PETUNIA. He wants you to stop singing it.

DUSTY. Yeah I know. But I like it. He's not gonna get angry at me over a song, is he?

PETUNIA. I think it's best not to give him a reason to be angry.

DUSTY. I think it's fine. What is he gonna do to me?

PETUNIA. Well –

DUSTY. Why are there kids in here?

PETUNIA. This is Bobo's niece and nephew. [or "nieces," or "nephews." Or "Bobo's their uncle."]

DUSTY. Oh. Oh! I didn't know. Oh hey kids, welcome. *(To the rest of the establishment.)* Hide the dildos! Put the guns out of sight. Maybe put the safety on. Hey! That's not okay! Stop that. There's some fucking kids in here. Petunia that reminds me, why are there kids in here?

PETUNIA. I don't know. Bobo just told me to watch them.

DUSTY. Why you?

PETUNIA. I don't know. I hate kids. No offense.

ZUZU. I take offense.

ZIPPY. I don't. But I'm a disaffected young clown. What's the Wi-Fi?

DUSTY. Oh yeah. Nothing works because of the snowstorm.

ZUZU. I hate snow.

PETUNIA. What? What kind of kid hates snow?

ZIPPY. I hate snow too. There's no school now to get cancelled anyway so what's the point? This is the worst Christmas vacation ever!

DUSTY. Hey now. I could sing again. Let me think if I know any appropriate songs. No. Not that one. No. No. No. Are you okay with the word "rim"?

(Rim shot sound effect.)

PETUNIA. Why don't I tell you a Christmas story? We should all get in a funny holiday spirit. Wouldn't that be nice? One year I was with a John. No maybe that's not appropriate. So this other year I was with these two Johns –

DUSTY. Petunia!

PETUNIA. What?

*(Enter **TIMMY**, covered in snow. He doesn't look so good.)*

TIMMY. Hi everybody.

PETUNIA. Timmy. You shouldn't be here right now.

TIMMY. No, I know. I thought maybe Bobo had some work for me.

PETUNIA. No work today.

TIMMY. Yeah but maybe I could pick something up or deliver something or maybe go tell someone they better pay up or else?

PETUNIA. Shotgun and Giggles got all that covered. Anyway, it's almost Christmas. Go home.

TIMMY. Yeah yeah. I will. I just need a little money. Petunia, you got any money?

PETUNIA. No. I'm flat broke. I don't know why they call it that. When I'm flat on my back, I'm not broke no more.

TIMMY. Dusty?

DUSTY. You know I don't give you money. "Don't ever lend and don't never borrow." You know who said that? Someone who's still alive. I'm trying to stay alive.

ZIPPY. I think that was Shakespeare.

ZUZU. What do you need money for?

PETUNIA. Kids, you don't need to...um.

TIMMY. Well kids, I got this friend, right? Frosty the Snowman. Actually looks kinda like Dusty in a different hat. Hey Dusty will you – Frosty's always like –

*(**DUSTY** changes into Frosty. Does he throw a sheet over himself – like a ghost costume? And put on a top hat? Or just the hat?)*

DUSTY. *(As Frosty.)* Hey. You got the money?

TIMMY. Frosty! You're alive! Was it some magic in the hat?

DUSTY. Yeah, something like that. Where's my money?

TIMMY. I'll get it. Can I just get a little more... *(Looks at kids.)* snow.

DUSTY. Not until I get my money.

TIMMY. Just a little taste. Just a little to tide me over.

DUSTY. No money, no snow.

TIMMY. I'm good for it.

DUSTY. If you were good for it, you'd have it.

TIMMY. I'll get it soon. Bobo will give me another job.

DUSTY. Until he does, don't call me, kid. Forget my name. The name's Frosty. That's the name you should forget.

TIMMY. But – but –!!

> *(**DUSTY** takes off the sheet – has it slowly melt in front of him until it's just a top hat on the ground on a sheet.)*

And then he melts and won't answer my texts anymore.

DUSTY. Sorry, Timmy.

TIMMY. What about you kids? You got any money?

ZIPPY. I got a dollar for you if you do a dance.

TIMMY. Nah, never mind.

ZIPPY. Two dollars.

TIMMY. No. Well... No.

ZIPPY. Five dollars?

TIMMY. Okay. Like, right now?

ZIPPY. Yeah. Do a Christmas dance.

TIMMY. What's a Christmas dance?

ZIPPY. Do it. Dance! Dance! Dance! Better! Do it better!

> (**TIMMY** *does a Christmas dance. When he's
> done,* **ZIPPY** *pays him. Exit* **TIMMY.***)*

TIMMY. *(On phone as he exits.)* Hey, Frosty?

ZUZU. That was sad.

ZIPPY. He smells bad too.

ZUZU. Every time a bell rings, a down-on-his-luck clown
dies.

DUSTY. That's dark.

PETUNIA. Maybe let's come up with like a happy story we
can tell.

DUSTY. What about the story of the mob boss, Bippineezer
Stooge?

PETUNIA. Well, I wouldn't call that hap–

> (**GIGGLES** *and* **SHOTGUN** *enter, both covered
> in snow.)*

GIGGLES. Bippineezer Stooge was ungenerous as the day
was long.

DUSTY. Oh hey Giggles. How did you know we were –

SHOTGUN. Please Mister Stooge. Can I git Christmas Day
off?

DUSTY. *(To* **SHOTGUN.***)* Oh Shotgun's playing Bobo Crachit.

GIGGLES. No. I need you to do the thing.

SHOTGUN. The thing?

GIGGLES. Yeh, the thing. The thing.

SHOTGUN. The thing. But it's Christmas! Please, sir!

GIGGLES. I don't care what day it is. Bah! Dicktug!

DUSTY. That night, Bippineezer is visited by his old partner Morey which is weird because he's dead.

PETUNIA. Ohh! Can I play it? *(Putting on a voice.)* Oooooh! I'm dead. You must change your ways. Clown criminals can't unionize but they need time off and better pay or else bad things could happen. Heed my warning. Three clowns will come. Threeee!

DUSTY. *(Sings.)*

I SAW THREE CLOWNS COME STUM—

PETUNIA. No.

DUSTY. *(We Three Kings tune.)*

WE THREE CLOWNS OF THE CLOWN BAR ARE

PETUNIA. No.

DUSTY. *(Sings.)*

ON THE THIRD DAY OF CHRISTMAS MY TRUE LOVE GAVE
TO ME.

PETUNIA. No.

DUSTY. *(Sings – instead of three french hens.)*

THREE MAD CLOWNS!

PETUNIA. Be very afraid Bippineezer! Repent! Change your ways!

GIGGLES. *(As Stooge.)* Yeh. I'm not worried about this. Three clowns. Whatever. Bah! Dicktug!

DUSTY. And he goes back to sleep. But then he wakes when there's a bang on his door.

SHOTGUN. Bang Bang Bang! Let me in! I'm a clown from your past.

GIGGLES. What da ya want?

SHOTGUN. Lookit who you used to be. Lookit the mistakes you made, the bad choices.

DUSTY. And he shows 'em.

SHOTGUN. I have this picture album you ken look at. Look. Look. Remember you were loved once.

GIGGLES. No.

PETUNIA. Bippineezer, you lost your way. We were going to marry once, weren't we? But you were too cheap.

GIGGLES. I made my choices!

SHOTGUN. Change now. Or else.

GIGGLES. I like my ways. Mostly. I think.

SHOTGUN. Okay, but, don't say I didn't warn ya.

DUSTY & PETUNIA. Don't say I didn't warn ya!

DUSTY. Then a while later there was another knock.

SHOTGUN. I am a clown from the present! Let me in! And know me better, man!

GIGGLES. What?

SHOTGUN. Lookit how everyone's having fun and you're not. Because you're a wet blanket.

GIGGLES. I don't care.

SHOTGUN. I think it would be good for you if you cared a little.

GIGGLES. I don't care.

SHOTGUN. But look at Bobo Crachit's family. Huddled by the fire.

PETUNIA. We are so poor.

DUSTY. So poor. But we are happy anyway, even though I am dying. *(Cough. Cough.)*

PETUNIA. Bobo, we need more money for our poor little son. Ask your boss for a raise.

DUSTY. I'm fine! *(Cough cough.)* I'll live a little longer, probably. God bless us, everyone.

GIGGLES. We all make choices.

SHOTGUN. He made a choice to work for you!

GIGGLES. Should have gone into business for himself. Didn't have the guts.

SHOTGUN. Listen to me. The third clown, not so fun. But take my advice now and it'll save you a lot of hurt. Seriously, before it's too late.

GIGGLES. Bah. I am me and I will not change in any appreciative way. I'm not even sure change is possible.

DUSTY & PETUNIA. Hmm.

(They all think if change is possible.)

SHOTGUN. Your loss, big guy.

DUSTY. And he goes back asleep but he's awoken by someone looming over him whilst he's in his bed.

GIGGLES. How'd you get in here? Why are you hiding your face? What clown are you? Are you here about my future?

DUSTY. But the clown does not speak. He just puts two in his head and one in his heart.

SHOTGUN. Bang. Bang. Bang.

*(**GIGGLES** takes a long time to die, loudly.)*

DUSTY. You done?

GIGGLES. Ugh. *(Bippineezer dies.)*

DUSTY. And that clown that done him in was Bobo Crachit. And that's how Bobo became the big boss.

PETUNIA. So what'd you kids think?

ZUZU. Meh.

ZIPPY. Wait. Is that how Bobo took over the Clown Bar?

SHOTGUN. Oh. That mighta been a secret.

GIGGLES. Yeah, don't tell any cops. You a snitch?

ZIPPY. No.

GIGGLES. You a snitch?

ZUZU. No.

GIGGLES. Good, then Bob's your uncle.

ZUZU. Bobo's my uncle.

SHOTGUN. Right, right. Now what? Want to hear about Hannaukuh Harry and the war against the Wilderness Wombat that almost ended in total annihilation of the human race?

PETUNIA. No, don't tell that one.

   (*Enter* **HAPPY**, *brushing off snow.*)

HAPPY. What's going on here?

GIGGLES. Hey, Happy. Still snowing?

ZUZU. That's Happy?

ZIPPY. He doesn't look like much.

ZUZU. No, he doesn't look like much.

SHOTGUN. What's the haps, Haps?

PETUNIA. Oh hi Happy. Blinky's not here.

HAPPY. No. I know. Why you bringing her up then?

PETUNIA. Usually you're looking for her right before her show. But I hadn't seen her today. Did you have a fight again?

HAPPY. Why would you say that?

SHOTGUN. Because you're always fighting.

GIGGLES. Yeh, it's true.

HAPPY. We're not, not that's not – it's just that. There's a distance between me and her. She's mysterious, shrouded in shadow. A goddess of light. And I'm just a regular joe.

PETUNIA. Nothin regular about you, not from what I heard.

GIGGLES. No, he's right about hisself. Happy's just some jerk, like the rest of us. You're not special.

SHOTGUN. You're not special.

GIGGLES. You're not special!

SHOTGUN. Blinky Fatale's special.

HAPPY. I know.

PETUNIA. Yeh you don't need that kinda stress. You know I'm a stress reliever. You want a drink? On the house. I know what you like. Rye. I always think W-R-Y when you say it because of how you are but I know it's really R-I-E. I'll make it extra funny. And I'll add a swizzle stick for extra izzle. *(Whispers.)* Izzle. Izzle.

HAPPY. *(Accepting drink.)* Thanks, Petunia!

PETUNIA. Look Happy, I'm all festive. I got mistletoe here and here and here. Come closer, I'll show you. *(She's about to try to kiss him.)*

HAPPY. Be careful, with the mistletoe, Petunia. That stuff's poisonous.

PETUNIA. *(Disappointed in a familiar yet devastating way.)* I know it. Love is poisonous.

HAPPY. What's with the kids?

SHOTGUN. Bobo's their uncle. We're getting them into the Christmas spirit.

GIGGLES. We're teaching them the true meaning of Christmas.

DUSTY. We're entertaining them 'cause there's no internet.

> *(Music starts up.)*

Oh is that what time it is already? Clowns and clowns, children and gangsters! Blinky's Christmas routine. Did she come in the back way? This song's about sex. Maybe kids shouldn't be in here. Oops. Too late. Close your eyes or somethin'.

> *(Sings, to "Jingle Bells," while* **BLINKY** *comes out and does her burlesque routine. Maybe the musical intro is long because the song is short.)*

DASHING THROUGH THE SNOW
IN A NEARLY NAKED WAY
ON THE STAGE WE GO
JIGGLING ALL THE DAY
HUH HUH HUH
BELLS ON EVERYTHING
MAKING SPIRITS BRIGHT
WHAT JOY IT IS TO PRANCE AND SING
A SEX CLOWN DANCE TONIGHT, OH!
JINGLE BELLS, JINGLE BELLS JINGLE THAT MY WAY
OH, WHAT FUN IT IS TO RIDE
WHEN IT'S ALL-KINK OPEN PLAY, HEY!

(Spoken:) Everybody!
JINGLE BELLS, JINGLE BELLS JINGLE THAT MY WAY
OH, WHAT FUN IT IS TO RIDE
WHEN IT'S ALL-KINK OPEN PLAY.

(Spoken:) Now just me.
NOW YOU KNOW I BITE
GET IT WHILE YOU'RE YOUNG
GRASP THE CLOWNS TONIGHT
SING THIS SEXY SONG
GET AN EASY LAY

A BRIDLE FOR YOUR STEED
AND HITCH HIM TO AN OPEN SLEIGH
AND YOU WILL TAKE THE LEAD
OHHHHHH
JINGLE BELLS, JINGLE BELLS JINGLE THAT MY WAY
OH, WHAT FUN IT IS TO RIDE
WHEN IT'S ALL-KINK OPEN PLAY, HEY!
JINGLE BELLS, JINGLE BELLS JINGLE THAT MY WAY
OH, WHAT FUN IT IS TO RIDE WHEN IT'S ALL-KINK OPEN PLAY!
WHEN IT'S ALL-KINK OPEN PLAYYYYY!

(**BLINKY**, *having finished her routine, puts on a robe.* **HAPPY** *goes over to her applauding but she gives him the cold shoulder.*)

BLINKY. Who brought kids?

HAPPY. Bobo.

BLINKY. Oh.

HAPPY. You looked good up there, Blinky.

BLINKY. Yeah. I always look good. What's it to ya?

HAPPY. You're not still mad, are you?

BLINKY. Do I look mad?

HAPPY. I think you might be.

BLINKY. If I'm mad, you made me mad, Happy.

HAPPY. I didn't mean to.

BLINKY. Where you been all week?

HAPPY. I was looking into something.

ZUZU. You know if you neglect your girl, she might not be there the next time you come around.

HAPPY What?

BLINKY. Listen to the kid.

ZUZU. Just saying. She reaches out, doesn't hear back from you, maybe next time she doesn't reach out. Maybe she'll reach out to someone else...

HAPPY. Okay, thanks.

ZUZU. Fine. I'm just trying to help. Like those three clowns helped Bippineezer Scrooge.

ZIPPY. Not so much the last one.

ZUZU. No, not so much the last one.

HAPPY. Okay well thanks, but I think I got it.

ZUZU. I don't think you do. Everyone here is right. You're out of your league.

HAPPY. *(To* **BLINKY**.*)* Can I talk to you in the back?

> *(Exit* **HAPPY** *and* **BLINKY**.*)*

PETUNIA. Okay, maybe it's time for another story.

> *(Enter* **POPO**, *terrifying, bloody, maybe carrying a chainsaw.)*

POPO. Did someone say storytime?

> *(Everyone reacts.)*

DUSTY. Where'd you come from?

GIGGLES. That was terrifying, Popo.

SHOTGUN. Yeah, that was real... I'm not afraid though.

POPO. Hi kiddies!

ZUZU & ZIPPY. Hi Aunt Popo.

PETUNIA. What are you doing, Popo? You got a job?

POPO. There's another hit but it's too snowy out. I would have had to walk and Popo hates to walk.

PETUNIA. Wait, do you kids know what a hit is?

ZIPPY. It's like a very successful song or TV show or product or I.P.

ZUZU. Popo kills people.

PETUNIA. Oh. Uh. You got a story, Popo? It's not too scary, right? Or gory. Like it won't give me nightmares? Is it okay for little ears to hear?

POPO. It's called The Snitch Who Stole Christmas!

DUSTY, SHOTGUN & GIGGLES. *(A dramatic sound effect.)* Dun dun!

> *(**GIGGLES** and **DUSTY** do a puppet show maybe with sock puppets to illustrate **POPO**'s story during the following.)*

POPO. Every clown down in Clowntown likes Christmas a lot.

The Snitch from the ditch in Frowntown, does not.

SHOTGUN. *(As Snitch, a green sock with google eyes.)* Yuck, Christmas.

POPO. The Snitch hates Christmas. It's just too funny.

The reindeers play dumb games and their noses are runny.

GIGGLES. *(As reindeer puppet.)* My glowing runny nose!

POPO. Some guys is just like that. They don't like to chuckle.

Can't get into the spirit. They're a sack of fuckos.

PETUNIA. Ahem.

POPO. Who can say why though? It's anybody's call. I think his clown nose is two sizes too small.

SHOTGUN. *(As Snitch.)* Ow, my nose.

POPO. Anyways, it's Christmas Eve and he hates all the clowns, singing and dancing, stumbling around. The Snitch from Frowntown doesn't like all the sounds.

DUSTY. *(Creating ambience.)*

FA LA LA LA LA, LA LA LA LA.

POPO. The clowns in Clowntown are having clown fights, committing clown crimes, carousing all night.

The Snitch says "If only there was a way to indict."

Then Christmas won't come. Won't that be a sight?

SHOTGUN. Yeh!

POPO. 'Cause on Christmas the clowns in Clowntown play tricks

Light fireworks, steal cars, swing sacks of bricks.

> *(Puppets do a version of this. Maybe set off one of those confetti poppers.)*

And they spend all day pieing each other in the face.

They pie the Snitch too if he's in the wrong place.

And then they all gather together and sing clowny songs

They sing and they sing and they sing all night long.

> *(**POPO** looks at **DUSTY**.)*

DUSTY.

DECK THE BAR WITH BOUGHS OF HOLLY
FA LA LA LA LA, LA LA LA LA
'TIS THE SEASON TO BE JOLLY
FA LA LA LA LA, LA LA LA LA

> *(**POPO** makes a cutting gesture and **DUSTY** stops.)*

POPO. The Snitch knew he had to stop Christmas this year

So he goes to his office and turns with a sneer

And flips through his papers for the proof that he had

That the clowns down in Clowntown were all very bad.

ALL. Boooo!

POPO. Yes, right. That's the correct sentiment.

The Snitch goes downtown to talk to the blue.

And there the Snitch rats you out.

And you and you and you.

Rats out every clown and all their dogs too.

SHOTGUN. *(As puppet dog.)* Rawr.

POPO. So the cops stomp around every home in Clowntown

Swinging their badges and their sticks around

Bashing in faces and doors and clowns

Taking them downtown in their nightgowns.

SHOTGUN. This is the coppers. Open up!

POPO. SWAT teams slide down the chimney right through the flue.

Even put cuffs on Little Cindy Lou Who.

SHOTGUN. Who?

POPO. Yeah.

They fill up the jails then they pack in two more.

GIGGLES. *(As puppet.)* Move over.

POPO. When they piss and they miss they piss on the floor.

Clowns overfilling out of every cop cage

Barely containing their simmering rage

The Snitch settles back in his house on the hill

He can hardly wait for his Christmas day thrill.

GIGGLES. *(As Snitch puppet.)* Yay!

POPO. He tucks himself in, so smug and so snug

And rolls himself up like a pug in a rug.

He weeps himself to sleep, with joy he weeps

And he pulls up the blankets and he

Sleeps sleeps sleeps sleeps

Until he's awoken by

Squeak, squeak, squeak, squeak

And the clomp clomp clomp clomp

of hundreds of clown feet

DUSTY.

FA LA LA LA LA, LA LA LA LA!

(Puppets celebrate.)

POPO. The clowns down in Clowntown let out a big
Christmas cheer

They set off their fireworks. They drink all their beer.

They dance in the streets, they throw all their pies.

Clowns are all out, clowns of all size

'Cause the thing about clown crime is that it's organized

They all made bail with a skip and a hop

Witnesses drop, charges are dropped

Guns in the night go pop pop pop pop.

And it's Christmas morning so they celebrate

Bring all the fun, leave all the hate

SHOTGUN. For later

POPO. Seltzer sprays and whoopee cushions and socks full of oranges

So many clowns come, they break the door hinges.

"How could this be?" the Snitch shouts in fear

"Maybe Christmas," he thinks "will always be here."

Like those clowns in Clowntown

And unlike Van Gogh's ear.

And the Snitch has to run cause his roast beast is cooked.

And he knows if they catch him, they'll have his neck on a hook.

So he ran runs runs runs.

He's still running to this day.

Or possibly sunk in the middle of the bay.

'Cause snitches are bitches who all have to pay.

The end.

(Everyone applauds, hoots and hollers.)

ZUZU. Thanks, Aunt Popo.

ZIPPY. Yeah, thanks, Aunt Popo.

POPO. All right. Keep your noses clean. Fuck it. I'm going out there. Crime never sleeps. And a little snow never stopped Popo.

> *(She picks up her chainsaw or straps herself with lots of weapons while everyone watches and puts on a pink hat with a pompom and then she exits.)*

PETUNIA. Did you kids really like that?

ZUZU. Yeah, why? What'd you hear

ZIPPY. I love Aunt Popo, but she's terrifying.

(Enter **BLINKY** and **HAPPY**, arguing.)

BLINKY. You know what your problem is, Happy?

HAPPY. What's my problem?

BLINKY. You don't know who you are. If you knew who you were you could see me more clearly for who I am.

HAPPY. Who are you?

BLINKY. I'm the cat's meow.

HAPPY. Well, I already knowed that, Blinky.

BLINKY. Well you don't act like it.

HAPPY. I've just been preoccupied lately.

BLINKY. With what? Why? What's your problem?

HAPPY. I thought you jus' told me what my problem was.

BLINKY. Maybe I don't know you as well as I thought.

HAPPY. I guess I just –

BLINKY. Spit it out.

HAPPY. I'm – maybe I'm confused. (Low.) About the clown life.

BLINKY. What about the clown life?

HAPPY. I don't think anything is funny anymore.

BLINKY. But it's Christmas. The funniest time of year.

HAPPY. I know. I just can't get into it.

BLINKY. You depressed? You gonna be a sad clown now?

HAPPY. No. I don't know.

BLINKY. You know what I think? I think you're just not sure about me.

HAPPY. No, that's not –

BLINKY. I have a sordid past wherein you've always been squeaky clean. Since birth. Above it all as a baby clown even. Surrounded by filth but none of it dare touch Happy Mahoney.

HAPPY. You're not bein' fair.

BLINKY. You're the one who's not being fair. You want a story? I got a story for you kids. It's called Blinky The Red Nosed Dancer.

> *(This is not sung.)*

Blinky, the red nosed dancer, had a very squeaky nose.

Honk Honk.

The other dancers, not impressed with this.

They would boo. They would hiss.

They would slut shame.

PETUNIA. *(Playing the part.)* You're not good at being a slut!

BLINKY. And call her bad names.

GIGGLES. Clowny!

PETUNIA. Seltzer puss!

SHOTGUN. You wear clown noses on your nipples too?

GIGGLES. Honk for me! Like a goose!

BLINKY. That's enough.

They never let her join in any dancing games.

GIGGLES. No clowns allowed!

BLINKY. Then one foggy holiday season

Without any real rhyme or reason

She wanders around downtown

Looking for a place to wave her wares around

She dances at Phil's

She dances at Bill's

She dances at Gil's and Mills and Still's

She dances at Shorty's. She dances at Talls.

By the end of the night she's danced at them all.

Except for one, an unmarked bar

Where she sees

clown after clown get out of a car.

GIGGLES. *(Playing a clown in the story.)* You know I don't even want to be a clown. I want to be an accountant. Why am I such a misfit?

PETUNIA. *(As herself.)* I kinda do want to be an accountant.

BLINKY. She follows the trail of glitter and grime

Into a bar thick with clown crime.

She dances all night, her nose all red

The word spreads when she spreads

Blinking under the glare, she is the star

They come from near. They come from far

to see fair Blinky Fatale at the Clown Bar

GIGGLES. I was going to have to close the bar this Christmas. Never to open again. But now people are coming. You saved us. You with your squeaky nose. You lit up the bar. You saved Christmas.

BLINKY. And you know who that was?

ZUZU. Santa Claus?

BLINKY. No. It was the bar owner.

ZIPPY. Uncle Bobo?

BLINKY. No, it was the previous owner. Bippineezer Stooge.

ZUZU. Oh. And did the other dancers come back and apologize for being so mean and tell you what a great dancer you were?

BLINKY. No.

ZIPPY. Did your boss give you a lot of money for saving the bar?

BLINKY. Not really. I guess I'm just still a lowly dancer who had to do other things to get by. Which is all Happy sees when he looks at me.

(**BLINKY**, *upset, starts to leave.*)

HAPPY. Wait, Blinky!

PETUNIA. Let her go.

HAPPY. Yeah, but –

PETUNIA. She needs a minute. You really don't understand lady clowns do you?

HAPPY. Why do you say that?

PETUNIA. Anyway, I need your help with my story.

HAPPY. Oh I'm not so good at that.

PETUNIA. Here I wrote down everything you need to say. (*Hands him a script.*)

HAPPY. Yeah, but –

ZUZU. Aren't we done with stories yet?

PETUNIA. No. This is my favorite Christmas story. Every year there's so many new Christmas movies but my very favorite is *The Christmas Tree Farm*. It's about a clown who leaves the big show to help run her grandfather's failing Christmas Tree Farm.

GIGGLES. Oh, granddaughter! It's so great you're here but can you leave behind the clown life like this?

PETUNIA. It's important to be here. Anyway –

PETUNIA, DUSTY & SHOTGUN. Once a clown, always a clown.

GIGGLES. I guess that's true.

PETUNIA. Anyway, I'm studying to be a tree doctor.

GIGGLES. A clown tree doctor?

PETUNIA. Yes.

GIGGLES. Good. I'm not sure what's wrong with these trees. They seem to whither.

PETUNIA. Whither?

GIGGLES. Hither.

PETUNIA. Have you tried telling them jokes?

GIGGLES. I always mean to but the days are long and I get so tired.

PETUNIA. That's why I'm here to help. *(Telling the jokes.)* Spruce yourselves up, friends! Stop needlin' me. Are you pining to be in someone's living room? Knock Knock. Why aren't you saying anything? Are you stumped? What's a tree's favorite sex position? Cone bone.

GIGGLES. I think it's working. I can feel them laughing.

PETUNIA. Also let's get some nitrogen and some fertilizer.

GIGGLES. You're a genius, granddaughter. And also a really good clown.

PETUNIA. I know.

SHOTGUN. And then one day she meets the handsome charming owner of the competing Christmas tree farm.

PETUNIA. That's you, Happy.

HAPPY. Oh, uh. Old man!

GIGGLES. Not you again. I'm not selling my farm to you.

HAPPY. I'll give you a good price.

PETUNIA. You leave my grandfather alone.

> (**HAPPY** *and* **PETUNIA** *look at each other.*
> *Magical music.**)

DUSTY. But then they look into each others' eyes. And
everything stops. They can hear their hearts beating.
Honk, honk. Honk, honk. Syncopated rhythm. They
breathe together and look deeply into each others' eyes.

HAPPY. Sorry. I didn't mean to cause a problem.

PETUNIA. Oh that's okay.

HAPPY. It's just that I love trees so much. Are you a clown
tree doctor?

PETUNIA. I am. I also love trees. And our tree farm.

HAPPY. Of course you do.

PETUNIA. Of course I do.

HAPPY. But if my tree farm fails, I'll have to go back to my
old life. Rodeo clown.

PETUNIA. You don't say.

HAPPY. Last bull charge almost did me in for good.

PETUNIA. Dangerous life. Not like trees.

HAPPY. No, not like trees. Unless they fall on you. Well
I should go. I'll see you around.

---

* A license to produce *Clown Bar Christmas* does not include a
performance license for any third-party or copyrighted music. Licensees
should create an original composition or use music in the public domain.
For further information, please see the Music and Third-Party Materials
Use Note on page iii.

PETUNIA. Yeah. See you maybe.

SHOTGUN. They fall into a competitive love hate relationship because all season long they have to fight for customers to keep their farms open.

HAPPY. Best trees here!

PETUNIA. Funnier trees over here. I got balsam fir. Won't get "fir" with those dumb pines at my competitor's farm.

HAPPY. What do you think you're doing?

PETUNIA. Running a business. What are you doing?

HAPPY. Better trees here! Don't buy slop. Your tree should pop!

SHOTGUN. It's a cutthroat business, the Christmas tree game. All day long, they compete, lob insults at each other. At night, they discard their competition. They build snowmen, skate on the pond, go ice-fishing, play hockey, sled, ride in a horse-drawn sleigh.

HAPPY. You're the most beautiful clown I've ever met.

PETUNIA. I know. You're nice to look at too. But our farms compete.

SHOTGUN. Then there's a misunderstanding.

PETUNIA. I heard what you said.

HAPPY. I don't know what you mean.

PETUNIA. I never want to see you again.

HAPPY. Fine!

PETUNIA. Fine!

SHOTGUN. And then her grandfather falls ill.

GIGGLES. Cough. Cough. It's over. Just sell the farm. It's not worth the stress.

PETUNIA. But what will you do? The farm is your whole life.

GIGGLES. I have other dreams. I've always wanted to make Easter baskets and run a costume store around Halloween.

PETUNIA. Okay, we'll sell to you. Are you happy?

HAPPY. Never. Not unless you agree to be my wife.

PETUNIA. But –

HAPPY. That misunderstanding was a misunderstanding. We'll combine the farms. You'll help the trees grow tall. I'll sell them at a higher price. Can you see it?

PETUNIA. I can see it. But the big show calls to me.

HAPPY. What about a small show?

PETUNIA. How small?

HAPPY. In the summer we'll have a tiny circus. Here at the combined farms. People will come from miles around. Clowns and regular folk.

       (**DUSTY** *hums circus song.*)

We'll have unicycles! Knife throwing. Trained animals. Very small cars full of clowns. Can you see it?

PETUNIA. I can see it.

HAPPY. What do you say?

PETUNIA. I do!

SHOTGUN. And they get married. And live happily ever after. In a Christmas paradise.

       (**PETUNIA** *is trying to kiss* **HAPPY** *again but he moves away.*)

HAPPY. Yep. Pretty good story, Petunia. I didn't know that one.

PETUNIA. They show it every year. On the Clownmark channel. You played that part really well, Happy. Didn't he?

ZIPPY. He was fine. What happened after that? Did he get gored by a bull at the Christmas tree farm circus?

PETUNIA. No, there were no bulls at their summer circus. Just tumbling and stuff. Strip shows.

ZIPPY. Shame.

ZUZU. Don't listen to Zippy. I liked it a lot Petunia.

HAPPY. Where's Blinky? I should go after her now, right?

> (**OLD SPATCHY** *enters covered in snow, maybe has a cane, definitely has a thick Eastern European accent.*)

OLD SPATCHY. Oh! My bones. Where can Old Spatchy sit?

ZUZU. What is happening?

SHOTGUN. I didn't think you would come this year, Old Spatchy.

OLD SPATCHY. You thought I was too old to move?

GIGGLES. No. No.

OLD SPATCHY. You thought Old Spatchy had died.

DUSTY. No.

OLD SPATCHY. And why not. We all die. Even you, Shotsha.

SHOTGUN. Not me. I'll live forever.

OLD SPATCHY. You know why Old Spatchy is here. It is almost Christmas and I must tell the story. Gigg, Shotsha, and even you, Dusty. You will perform the story.

HAPPY. Do you want me to –

OLD SPATCHY. No. Petunksa, you will do the snow dance.

PETUNIA. Yes, okay, right. Sure.

> (**PETUNIA** *does a sort of ballet.*)

OLD SPATCHY. Snow!

> (*The others make it snow.*)

One day, yes. It is. Okay. Cold. The snowfall like no snowfall and it do not stop. You know? And so the snow it piles up until it reaches the window. And then more. The snow it climbs. And the villages are buried in the snow. Soon, you can not see the chimneys even. The smoke comes from holes in the snow. Okay? It is snowy. Okay? Yes. Snowy? Yes. Snowy? Yes.

ZUZU. Snowy.

OLD SPATCHY. They get it. Stop.

> (*The dance and snow stops abruptly.* **PETUNIA** *and* **SHOTGUN** *put on scarves and huddle. They take on the role of Father and Mother.*)

In one little house in the village –

SHOTGUN. Mother, it is so cold.

PETUNIA. Yes, Father. We shiver.

SHOTGUN. Will it never end?

PETUNIA. We will die after a time if the snow does not stop.

SHOTGUN. We have the canned goods?

PETUNIA. Yes, but they will not last.

SHOTGUN. We have the dried Morkodol.

PETUNIA. Yes but it will not last.

SHOTGUN. We have the hope for a better tomorrow.

PETUNIA. It will not last.

OLD SPATCHY.   Father looks at Mother suspiciously. Mother hopes he can not read her thoughts. Mother hopes he does not see in her bones. Father shakes his head.

PETUNIA. We could whistle.

> *(They whistle over the following.* **BLINKY** *enters from the back during this and watches.)*

OLD SPATCHY.   But she does not want to whistle. She wants to cut herself open and exorcise her Dodgot. She thinks if she whistles he will not look into her bones. She thinks it will delay the inevitable.

SHOTGUN. That was a good whistle, Mother.

PETUNIA. We are not done yet.

> *(***PETUNIA*** whistles more.* **SHOTGUN** *eventually joins in.)*

OLD SPATCHY.   In another house, not far from this house, a man does not exactly hear the whistle, but he feels it in his liver. It vibrates in his intestine.

> *(***GIGGLES*** perks up.)*

GIGGLES. What is this? Oh...so sad.

OLD SPATCHY.   Mother, in her feminineness, feels the man feel her. And at once, she knows it is her lover across the pond. The whistling does not quite carry through the snow across the small frozen pond through the unwalkable snow. But the sexiness does.

GIGGLES. My lover!

OLD SPATCHY.   Immediately she stops whistling.

SHOTGUN. Why have you stopped whistling, Mother?

OLD SPATCHY. She has no answer. She says nothing and then in the nothing she doesn't say, he thinks he hears something but he does not know what and anyway he is a man.

SHOTGUN. Oh well. I bet it was nothing.

(The scene ends and they begin to set up the next scene.)

OLD SPATCHY. You kids. You are enjoying?

ZIPPY. Um. Yes?

ZUZU. I think we have to.

OLD SPATCHY. Good. Duty. Yes? Hope. Yes? Community, no?

ZIPPY. Yes?

OLD SPATCHY. Far away in another frozen desert, Sata prepares for the holiday.

ZUZU. Sata?

OLD SPATCHY. Yes. Sata Nick.

ZIPPY. Santa?

OLD SPATCHY. Yes. Sata. Papa Christmas Sexytime.

*(**GIGGLES** appears dressed sort of like Santa but also not at all. **PETUNIA** as Ms. Santa, sort of.)*

Sata and the elbs.

(The other actors get on their knees to play elves.)

GIGGLES. HO! I am Sata! Fear me! HO!

OLD SPATCHY. And Mother Sata.

PETUNIA. I am Mother Sata! Fear me!

GIGGLES. We come to punish the bad children with sores and boils.

PETUNIA. We put spiders in your bed and neelies in your ear.

GIGGLES. We give you night scaries and leprosy.

PETUNIA. Your teeth fall out.

PETUNIA & GIGGLES. Fear us!

ZUZU. Is that only for bad kids?

OLD SPATCHY. Yes, bad kids.

ZIPPY. What about good kids.

OLD SPATCHY. I don't understand.

ZUZU. Don't they get presents?

OLD SPATCHY. Yes, sometimes if the child is very good and the parents are rich. Child gets socks and fruit.

ZIPPY. Is that all?

OLD SPATCHY. Rocks.

ZUZU. Pretty rocks?

OLD SPATCHY. No. Or sticks.

ZIPPY. And toys.

OLD SPATCHY. No.

ZUZU. I thought it was a Christmas story. Don't the kids get toys?

> (**OLD SPATCHY** *and* **SHOTGUN** *talk for a while in* **OLD SPATCHY***'s language. An animated conversation.*)

OLD SPATCHY. Michta kochev Vick Sata. Lood du vik. Toyshissh.

SHOTGUN. Kinder figitsh la doo. Re migin stoodod. Col vistatudik.

OLD SPATCHY. Nah nah nah nah. Ve krude la trutff.

SHOTGUN. Mitun. Sa kee.

(This goes on for a bit if you want.)

OLD SPATCHY. Okay. Kids get rocks.

SHOTGUN. And toys.

OLD SPATCHY. Okay. And toys.

PETUNIA & GIGGLES. Fear us! Fear us!

OLD SPATCHY. And then –

DUSTY. *(As elf.)* Sata.

GIGGLES. Yes, my short one.

DUSTY. There is a problem with the sky.

GIGGLES. What sort of problem?

DUSTY. Someone has taken it.

PETUNIA & GIGGLES. NOOOO!

OLD SPATCHY. Without a sky there will be no sky travel. Without a sky, perhaps the world will end. Perhaps there is no meaning to anything, no reason to go on. No reason to eat or breathe or take out the trash.

ZIPPY. There would be no Christmas?

OLD SPATCHY. Eh... Okay.

ZUZU. Is that what you're saying?

OLD SPATCHY. Okay.

ZIPPY. Wait. What do you mean, no sky?

OLD SPATCHY. The sky is not there. They look up and nothing.

ZUZU. Was it night?

ZIPPY. Maybe it was just dark and it looked like there was no sky.

OLD SPATCHY. No. It is poof. Someone take it.

ZUZU. I don't understand.

OLD SPATCHY. Do you not know the story of the missing sky?

ZUZU. Um, no. What?

OLD SPATCHY. Lucky. I wish I was you. To see it for the first time. A delight. A treat. Like a child on Christmas morning. The anticipation. The excitement. Now they do the dance of the missing sky and that should make everything clear.

GIGGLES. Do we have to?

OLD SPATCHY. Dance! There is no choice!

>   (*The clowns do the dance of the missing sky.
>   And then it is over.*)

Okay. Now I am tired and I go home.

ZUZU. Wait, what happened?

OLD SPATCHY. Did you not watch the dance?

ZUZU. Yeah, but.

OLD SPATCHY. Okay. And there is a sky above us now so you understand.

>   (*Exit* **OLD SPATCHY**, *hobbling with cane.
>   Groaning as they leave.*)

ZIPPY. So what was that?

DUSTY. It's a tradition.

ZIPPY. Yeah, but is it, though?

DUSTY. I mean it happens every year around Christmas, so yeah.

SHOTGUN. I didn't think she'd [or he'd, etc.] come. I thought last year was the last year.

HAPPY. Blinky, that was me. That story.

BLINKY. I don't know what you're talking about.

HAPPY. Whether there's a sky or not. Whether we're far away across a frozen wasteland or if it just feels like that, I see how beautiful your soul is. I know who you are and it's not about where you've been. We are lovers connected across walls of snow. I hear your whistle echo inside me.

BLINKY. That's the most romantic thing anyone's ever said to me.

HAPPY. You're the most important thing to me, Blinky.

BLINKY. You promise, Happy?

HAPPY. I promise. You'll always come first.

PETUNIA. As long as you come, it doesn't really matter the order. I'm multiorgasmic. And fun at birthday parties.

BLINKY. Oh Happy!

HAPPY. Oh Blinky! Let's never argue again.

(**HAPPY** and **BLINKY** as they do, start making out, going at it in front of everyone.)

DUSTY. (Sings. Note the word changes.)
SHOULD AULD ACQUAINTANCE BE FORGOT
AND NEVER BROUGHT TO MIND?
SHOULD AULD ACQUAINTANCE BE FORGOT
AND DAYS OF AULD LANG SYNE?

FOR AULD LANG SYNE, MY DEAR
FOR AULD LANG SYNE
WE'LL TAK A CUP O' KINDNESS YET
FOR DAYS OF AULD LANG SYNE

WE TWA HAE RUN ABOUT THE BAR

AND PU'D THE BEER TAP FINE
BUT WE'VE WANDER'D MONY A WEARY FIT
SIN DAYS OF AULD LANG SYNE

AND WE TWA HAE NAKED IN THE BAR
FRAE MORNING SUN 'TIL DINE
BUT SEAS BETWEEN US BRAID HAE ROAR'D
SIN DAYS OF AULD LANG SYNE

FOR AULD LANG SYNE, MY DEAR
FOR AULD LANG SYNE
WE'LL TAK A CUP O' KINDNESS YET
FOR DAYS OF AULD LANG SYNE

AND SURELY YE'LL BE YOUR PINT-STOWP
AND SURELY I'LL BE MINE
AND WE'LL TAK A CUP O' KINDNESS YET
FOR AULD LANG SYNE

AND THERE'S A HAND, MY TRUSTY CLOWN
AND GIE'S A HAND O' THINE
AND WE'LL TAK A RIGHT GUDE-WILLY FUCK
FOR AULD LANG SYNE

FOR AULD LANG SYNE, MY DEAR
FOR AULD LANG SYNE
WE'LL TAK A CUP O' KINDNESS YET
FOR AULD LANG SYNE
FOR AULD LANG SYNE, MY DEAR
FOR AULD LANG SYNE
WE'LL TAK A CUP O' KINDNESS YET
FOR AULD LANG SYNE

BLINKY. Let's go now. Run off together. Before it's too late.

HAPPY. Why would it be too late?

BLINKY. Bobo wants to talk to me. I'm not sure it's the kind of conversation I want to have. I wasn't sure about you and I was going to entertain all comers.

PETUNIA. I always entertain all comers.

BLINKY. But you and I could just go now. And never look back.

HAPPY. Sure. Sure. Let me just tell my Christmas story before I go. My favorite.

BLINKY. Not your favorite. Come on, Happy.

HAPPY. In a minute. I feel compelled by something bigger than me. Maybe it's the Christmas spirit within me or maybe – Anyway. It's a classic Christmas story. "Kill Hard."

SHOTGUN. It's not a Christmas story.

HAPPY. It is a Christmas story.

SHOTGUN. It's not.

HAPPY. It is!

SHOTGUN. Not!

HAPPY. Is!

GIGGLES. Police-a-ganda is what it is.

HAPPY. Quiet. Let me tell it.

(He tells this in a noir parody style.)

Christmas Eve in California. The first thing to know is that he's a cop but he's off his beat. He is a New York dick.

PETUNIA. I like New York dick.

HAPPY. The second thing to know is that his wife was estranged. He's there to visit her and their kids. For Christmas. She works in a tower in the heart of L.A. Corporate job, you know the kind.

ZUZU. What kind of corporation?

HAPPY. I don't know. Big money. Investing.

ZIPPY. Do they make whoopee cushions?

HAPPY. Okay. They make whoopee cushions.

ZIPPY. I love whoopee cushions.

HAPPY. He's there to visit his wife.

BLINKY. You don't got to be a cop in New York. Come back and live here with me. You don't got to be threatened because I got a nice office and am successful.

HAPPY. But I belong in New York. I'm a New York cop.

BLINKY. You could be an L.A. cop.

HAPPY. Nah. Things are all slippery here. Slimy. Also why didn't you keep my last name.

BLINKY. Take off your shoes. Get changed for the party.

HAPPY. It was a Christmas party. But something isn't right. Machine gun shots ring out.

SHOTGUN & GIGGLES. Bang bang bang bang!

HAPPY. It's a heist. They're terrorists who want money. So he climbs the elevator shafts and crawls through the ventilator shafts with only his trusty zippo to light the way.

ZIPPY. What?

ZUZU. He said Zippo, not Zippy. Zippy thought you were calling his [or her, etc] name.

ZIPPY. My name is Zippy.

HAPPY. I had an Uncle Zippy.

ZIPPY. Yeah it's a really common name.

ZUZU. Just finish the story.

HAPPY. So he hides in the bowels of the skyscraper. A game of cat and mouse. But who is the cat and who is the mouse? He takes out the terrorists one at a time. With only his brains and the guns he manages to collect. The phones are out so he steals a radio to call the cops.

SHOTGUN. This is the cops! Hello? No way is something happening. It's just a Christmas party with occasional machine gun fire.

HAPPY. It's a heist and terrorist action.

SHOTGUN. Seems like a normal night.

HAPPY. So he drops a dead terrorist on the the police car sent to investigate.

SHOTGUN. Oh, maybe something is going on.

HAPPY. But then the cops in charge don't believe what he's telling them so they do a lot of stupid things.

GIGGLES. Yeah. Cops are stupid.

HAPPY. It's a battle of brains between our guy and Hands Grabber, the terrorist leader.

GIGGLES. I'm all Hands! I will fuck you up!

SHOTGUN. This is the cops! What do you want?

GIGGLES. We want ten thousand pizzas delivered within thirty minutes.

SHOTGUN. That seems normal.

HAPPY. But our hero was much smarter. *(As him.)* Something's going on. They're not going to eat all those pizzas.

GIGGLES. Let's chase each other around and shoot at each other.

> (**GIGGLES**, **SHOTGUN**, **HAPPY**, *and maybe others run around shouting "Bang Bang Bang." They somersault, duck and cover, dive behind tables.)*

HAPPY. Yippee Kie Yay You Sons Of Bitches!

GIGGLES, SHOTGUN & HAPPY. Bang! Bang! Bang! Bang! Bang! Bang! Bang!

HAPPY. Our hero performs fantastic feat after fantastic feat.

GIGGLES. Big explosion! Big explosion!

SHOTGUN. Good thing the sprinklers in the building work well.

GIGGLES. The Christmas tree falls over.

HAPPY. After taking out almost all the bad guys, our hero shows up barefoot, limping, shouting, "Hands! Hands!"

> (**GIGGLES** *pretends* **BLINKY** *is the hero's wife, arm around her, fingers pointed like a gun to her head.*)

GIGGLES. Put the gun down! You think you're some kind of cowboy? You're nothing! I will shoot her. Put down the gun.

HAPPY. *(Holds his hands up.)* I'm unarmed.

SHOTGUN. But he has taped a holster to his back where Hands can't see. Bang. Bang.

> (**HAPPY** *mimes shooting.*)

GIGGLES. *(Pretends to fall from the tower.)* Ahhhh!

HAPPY. Hands falls and falls. Perhaps he's still falling to this day.

SHOTGUN. Maybe now his wife isn't as estranged as she was before.

BLINKY. My hero! I will take your last name.

> (**BLINKY** *and* **HAPPY** *kiss. It goes on a while.*)

ZIPPY. Okay. We get it.

HAPPY. There's a sequel too.

SHOTGUN. Sequels are dumb. All the cool characters are dead.

BLINKY. I don't really get it. Why do you like that story so much?

HAPPY. I think I want to be a cop.

(Everyone gasps.)

BLINKY. What?

HAPPY. Nothing. Nevermind.

BLINKY. What did you say?

GIGGLES. Don't ever say that again.

*(Enter **BOBO** from the back, dressed as a clown Santa Claus.)*

BOBO. Ho, ho ho!

PETUNIA. Bobo!

GIGGLES & SHOTGUN. Bobo!

BLINKY & HAPPY. Bobo.

BOBO. I'm Santa Claus.

ZIPPY. Hi Santa Claus. What'd you bring me?

BOBO. Did you kids have fun out here?

ZIPPY & ZUZU. Yes, Uncle Bobo.

ZIPPY. We told Holiday stories.

ZUZU. We learned the true meaning of Christmas.

BOBO. What's the true meaning of Christmas?

ZUZU. Um. Give unto others.

ZIPPY. Especially drug addicts.

ZUZU. Be generous to your employees.

ZIPPY. That's how you got this bar.

ZUZU. Don't snitch.

ZIPPY. Yeah. What else?

ZUZU. Don't be mean to someone who might someday save your bar. If possible fall in love in a small town and start a small circus on a Christmas tree farm. Then something about a stolen sky. Also public displays of affection are okay when everyone in the room is invested in your relationship. And then I guess um. Something about cops or.

ZIPPY. Just don't mess with Happy.

ZUZU. Yeah don't mess with Happy.

BOBO. You were busy.

ZIPPY. Yeah so what'd you get me, Santa?

BOBO. *(Reaching into his bag.)* A savings bond. In twenty years this will be worth something.

ZIPPY. Is that it? What about that game I wanted, Grand Clown Larceny.

BOBO. *(Giving small gift.)* Maybe just open this little gift and see what it is?

ZIPPY. Is it Grand Clown Larceny? 'Cause that's what I asked for and if it's not that...

BOBO. That's what it is.

ZIPPY. Okay. Thank you Uncle Bobo! You're the best!

BOBO. I know.

ZUZU. What did I get? A twin barrel carbon fiber airsoft rifle with laser sights and removable stock?

BOBO. You'll shoot your eye out, kid.

ZUZU. What?

BOBO. Just kidding. Here you go. *(Giving large gift.)*

ZUZU. Thank you, Uncle Bobo!

ZIPPY. We love you Uncle Bobo!

BOBO. Aw shucks. I guess I am lovable. You kids go wait in the car.

ZUZU. Okay. Bye everyone!

ZIPPY. Yeah.

>   (**ZUZU** and **ZIPPY** exit.)

BOBO. Shotgun, Giggles, did you finish all your errands?

SHOTGUN. Nah. Almost. Only one or two still to do. We'll go now.

GIGGLES. Even though there's snow and it's Christmas.

BOBO. I'll have a Christmas bonus for you both. When you get back.

GIGGLES. In that case, I guess.

BOBO. Get out of here!

>   (**SHOTGUN** and **GIGGLES** exit.)

Happy.

HAPPY. Bobo.

BOBO. Where were you? You weren't around. Blinky was missing you.

HAPPY. I was visiting a school.

BOBO. What kind of school?

BLINKY. Happy?!! A school!?

HAPPY. Don't worry about it. I was just thinking about a new career.

BOBO. That right? I was always hoping you'd come work for me. You think you want to do that?

HAPPY. I don't expect so.

BOBO. It could be the start of something special.

HAPPY. I think I have a different path.

BLINKY. Happy, what do you mean?

HAPPY. I, uh...

BOBO. Blinky, want to come into my office and finish that conversation we were having?

BLINKY. Oh. Well. Maybe tomorrow. I got to go. It's Christmas.

BOBO. Right. Christmas. Merry Christmas.

(*Exit* **BOBO** *after a tense stare at them both.*)

HAPPY. If I was smart, I'd follow him and finish him right now.

BLINKY. Are you smart, Happy?

HAPPY. I don't think so, Blinky.

BLINKY. You leaving Happy? Leaving us all behind.

HAPPY. No. I don't know. I haven't decided anything.

BLINKY. About me, you mean.

HAPPY. Stop that now. Let's enjoy Christmas.

BLINKY. You want to come home with me.

HAPPY. Course I do.

BLINKY. All right, Happy. I know you'll leave me. Good things never last. But tonight. Tonight, you're all mine.

HAPPY. Stop that now. You're my girl. Now and forever. All right?

BLINKY. All right.

(*Exit* **BLINKY** *and* **HAPPY.**)

PETUNIA. I could be his girl.

DUSTY. What's that?

PETUNIA. Nothing.

DUSTY. I think I'm gonna keep singing that song Bobo doesn't like. See what happens.

PETUNIA. And I'm gonna keep Christmas in my heart year round. There's lotsa room in there. It's so empty. Merry Christmas, Dusty.

DUSTY. Happy New Year, Petunia. All right! Everyone out! Bar's closed!

>   *(Sings.)*

WE WISH YOU A MERRY CHRISTMAS
WE WISH YOU A MERRY CHRISTMAS
WE WISH YOU A MERRY CHRISTMAS
JUST NOT RIGHT HERE!

GOOD TIDINGS WE BRING TO YOU AND YOUR CLOWNS
WE WISH YOU A MERRY CHRISTMAS
BUT GET OUT OF TOWN!

OH, BRING US SOME FUNNY PUDDING
OH, BRING US SOME FUNNY PUDDING
OH, BRING US SOME FUNNY PUDDING
BUT FIRST LEAVE MY BAR!

GOOD TIDINGS WE BRING TO YOU AND YOUR CLOWNS
WE WISH YOU A MERRY CHRISTMAS
BUT GET OUT OF TOWN!

YOU MUST GO BEFORE I GET MAD
YOU MUST GO BEFORE I GET MAD
YOU MUST GO BEFORE I GET MAD
SO GET OUTTA HERE

WE ALL LIKE OUR FUNNY PUDDING
WE ALL LIKE OUR FUNNY PUDDING
WE ALL LIKE OUR FUNNY PUDDING
WITH ALL ITS GOOD CHEERS

GOOD TIDINGS WE BRING TO YOU AND YOUR CLOWNS

WE WISH YOU A MERRY CHRISTMAS
BUT GET OUT OF TOWN!

WE WISH YOU A MERRY CHRISTMAS
WE WISH YOU A MERRY CHRISTMAS
WE WISH YOU A MERRY CHRISTMAS

AND A CLOWNY NEW YEAR!

> *(The whole cast has come out for the end of this and was singing the last half or two thirds of the song. This is also the curtain call.)*

End of Play

9 780573 711152